Dancing with Katya

Dori Chaconas

Illustrated by
Constance R. Bergum

PEACHTREE
ATLANTA

In loving memory of my mother,
Kathryn Baratka Kozak

—D. C.

In memory of my father Andy Rummel
and Kenny Coughlin, best friends and roommates
in the children's polio ward at St. Vincent's Hospital.

—C. B.

Ω

Published by
PEACHTREE PUBLISHERS
1700 Chattahoochee Avenue
Atlanta, Georgia 30318-2112

www.peachtree-online.com

Text © 2006 by Dori Chaconas
Illustrations © 2006 by Constance R. Bergum

Book design by Constance Bergum and Loraine M. Joyner

Illustrations created in watercolor on archival 100% rag paper. Title created
with Goudy Infant from dtpTypes Limited and Zapfino from Linotype
Library GmbH. Text typeset in Goudy Infant with Zapfina initial capitals.
Author and illustrator notes typeset in Adobe's Minion.

Printed in Singapore
10 9 8 7 6 5 4 3 2 1
First Edition

ISBN 1-56145-376-5

Library of Congress Cataloging-in-Publication Data
[CIP info to follow}

*B*efore my sister Katya could even walk, she loved to dance. She'd hold her baby arms out to me and I'd swoop her up, light as a seed puff, and twirl her around and around.

"Look, Mama! Look, Papa! I'm dancing with Katya!"

"Anna!" Mama would call. "Don't spin too fast!"

But she and Papa would laugh, watching. And best of all, Katya would laugh.

We danced together when Katya was two. We danced when she was three and when she was four. Then, late in the summer after she'd turned five, Katya got sick.

Doctor Mackey's horse and buggy sat in our farm yard day after day. I overheard the whispered words *high fever* and *crippled*.

Papa and Mama took turns sitting with Katya through the cooling nights. I heard her soft, mewing cries, like a kitten that'd lost its mama.

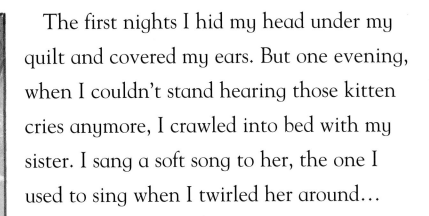

The first nights I hid my head under my quilt and covered my ears. But one evening, when I couldn't stand hearing those kitten cries anymore, I crawled into bed with my sister. I sang a soft song to her, the one I used to sing when I twirled her around…

Dancing with my Katya,
Dancing 'round and 'round.
Dance with me, my Katya—
Waltz your toes across the ground…

…until we both fell asleep.

In the morning, Mama was angry with me. She said I was not to sleep with Katya

or even go into the room with her or I might get sick, too. Papa gave me a hug and told me that Katya would get better. He said her strong will would take up where her puny body left off. He called it her "pioneer spirit."

Well into winter, Katya did get better. But the sickness had left her legs weak and sorely shaped. Papa made crutches, but they didn't help much. Mostly I just carried her. Even though she was six years old, Katya scarcely weighed more than a sack of potatoes.

"Can we go to the pond?" Katya asked on the first warm spring day. "Please, Anna! The chickens are fed, and the eggs are collected. Mama won't mind."

"And what would we do at the pond, Little Miss Kat?" I teased her.

She laughed. "You know!"

I put my little sister in the wheelbarrow and zigzagged over every bump I could find. Katya hung on to the sides. The cows watched as Kat rolled by, her laughter rising up, up, up until I thought it would brush the bottom of the sky.

When we sat in the new grass near the pond, Katya said, "Tell me about the picture, Anna. The picture in your teacher's book."

"Okay," I began, same as always. "The picture in Miss Kochik's book is called *The Dance Class*. It was painted by a French artist named Edgar Degas."

This had always been our favorite game. We'd talk about the picture, then pretend we were the ballerinas from the book. "The dancers wear satin slippers, with ribbons tied 'round their ankles," Katya finished.

Then I danced for Kat, a make-believe ballet, my feet and toes kissing the shaded grass. "Anna, will I ever be able to dance again?" she asked.

"You will," I answered. Then I picked Katya up and swirled her around until we both were laughing.

But I didn't know how such skinny, crooked legs could learn to dance when they couldn't even walk. I wondered if her pioneer spirit would be strong enough to make that happen.

One day in middle-summer, when mosquitoes buzzed in our ears and potato bugs chomped on plant leaves, Mama came home from town with a new cotton nightgown for Katya.

"I'm taking you to Minneapolis," she told Kat, "to a hospital, where doctors will make your legs strong." Katya looked at me, her eyes big with questions.

"We'll be gone a long time," Mama said. "A month or more. Aunt Mary will stay here to help Papa and Anna." Then Mama sent us out to

hunt for potato bugs before any questions could slide out of our mouths.

I duck-walked between the rows of plants. Katya scooted along behind me. "Here's three bugs, Anna," she said. "All on one leaf!"

Puk! Puk! Puk! She dropped each potato bug into a coffee can. The bugs stuck in the bacon grease Mama had slathered in the bottom of the can so they couldn't fly out again. Then Kat's voice changed to almost a whisper.

"What will the doctors do to my legs?" she asked.

"I don't know," I told her honestly.

"I don't want to go, Anna," she said. "I'm scared."

We sat between the rows, pressed together.

"Don't think about it, Kat," I told her. "Just think about dancing. After your legs are fixed we'll dance together, for real."

But I was scared, too.

I rode along in the wagon as Papa drove Mama and Katya to the train station. We had one last hug, one last wave good-bye. Then the train took Katya away from me for the very first time.

I cried that night, alone in our room.

Summer moved toward fall. Barn kittens grew into cats. Pond ducklings grew almost as big as their mothers. I went to the pond alone. The days stretched long.

*O*ne day a letter came from Mama. She wrote three pages of words, but the ones I remembered best were
Katya is walking.
I raced to the pond, swooping and flying like the tree swallows over my head. Katya was walking!

I danced with my arms whipping the sky and my feet driving the happy news into the ground. Katya was walking!

I whooped and laughed and shouted to the ducks, "Kat is walking!"

Kat's pioneer spirit had pushed the weakness right out of her legs.

*F*inally the day arrived when Katya and Mama would come home. I rode to the train station with Papa. The pictures in my mind opened like pages in a book: Katya would jump off the high step of the train. She would run to me and I'd swing her around and around.

"There she is, Papa!" I yelled over the train's noisy screeching and hissing.

But Kat didn't jump down. She didn't run to me. Papa lifted her from the high step, and then I saw her legs.

Katya wore heavy leather boots, laced all the way up to her knees. Metal braces, clamped to the boots, locked up her legs like cages. When Papa put her down, she swung each stiff leg forward. She walked like a toy tin soldier from the five-and-dime store.

She came to me and I tried to smile. But all the happiness inside me had turned as sour as pig slop. All our talk about Katya dancing was nothing but a lie. Katya's eyes burned with disappointment behind fast-coming tears.

"They didn't give me dancing shoes!" she said. "I'll never be able to dance in these ugly things!"

We celebrated Kat's homecoming at supper. Mama told about Minneapolis and the hospital. Papa told how many bushels of corn he'd picked. Katya looked worn out after her trip from Minneapolis. I watched her pick at her food. Her hands moved like butterflies searching for the sweetest flowers.

All through the next days, Katya carried a sadness around with her. It was as if her pioneer spirit had gotten lost somewhere between Minneapolis and home. More than anything, I wanted to find a way to make her sadness go away.

On market day, I begged Papa to take me to town with him. In one pocket I carried pennies I had saved. In the other pocket, I'd tucked a sewing needle wrapped in a scrap of paper with a twist of thread.

Papa went to the feed store. I went to the five-and-dime and bought what I needed. Then I sat in the wagon, my head bent, and worked with the needle and thread.

That afternoon, I took Katya to the pond. She rode in the wheelbarrow because she couldn't walk far on her own yet. I rolled the wheelbarrow over a bump or two, but when Kat looked uncomfortable from the joggling, I slowed and chose the smoothest way.

I wondered if Katya would still ask to play our favorite game. She settled onto the grass, her eyes skimming over the pond with an empty look in them.

I waited. And I waited some more. This was not working out the way I'd hoped it would. "Kat," I began, "maybe we should go back—"

But she interrupted me, her voice as soft as kitten fur. "Will you tell me about the picture again, Anna?"

"I will," I said. "But first, I have something for you," I said. I pulled the small paper sack from my pocket and spilled out a pair of dainty white gloves. There were tiny pearl buttons decorating the tops, and tangles of long, pink ribbons I had stitched on.

I slipped the gloves onto Katya's hands. I twisted and turned the shiny ribbons up her arms to her elbows and tied them in a bow, watching the sadness in her face turn to delight.

She looked so beautiful with her hands in ballerina gloves!

Then I started to dance. Katya stood up and watched. Soon her body swayed with mine. Her heavy boots even moved a bit above the grass, and her hands!

Oh…her hands! Kat's hands danced in the snatches of sunlight like white butterflies with pink satin tails. They flitted and fluttered through the golden air. They swirled and swooped, creating a magical painting more beautiful than any in Miss Kochik's book.

"Look, Anna!" she said, her smile shining with wonder and joy. "I'm dancing!"

And then I knew. Just as weak barn kittens grew into strong barn cats, Katya would grow and get strong. Just as pond ducklings grew wings strong enough to lift their bodies off the pond, Katya's legs would grow strong enough to walk, and even dance.

So we danced, each in our own way. The sun dapples danced, and the shadows danced. And we danced, on and on and on…

Dancing with my Katya,
Dancing 'round and 'round.
Someday your feet will waltz with mine
and fly across the ground.

AUTHOR'S NOTE

*Y*ears ago, polio was a feared illness. The polio virus attacked the nerve cells that make the body muscles work. When muscles can't work, they grow weak and useless. Many cases of polio were no worse than a bout of the flu. But some cases were severe and long lasting. Sometimes the virus even weakened the muscles that help a person breathe. Many polio victims had to be placed in a machine called an "iron lung" to help them breathe.

At first people called the disease *infantile paralysis.* They chose the word "infantile" because the virus primarily struck infants or children, and the word "paralysis" because it sometimes left the victim's muscles totally unable to move.

Adults could be stricken with polio, too. Our thirty-second president, Franklin Delano Roosevelt, came down with polio when he was thirty-nine years old. He had to use a wheelchair for the rest of his life.

In the 1950s, Doctors Jonas Salk and Albert Sabin developed successful vaccines to prevent polio. Scientists hope that polio will remain a disease of the past.

*K*athryn Baratka Kozak was born in 1910 on a small farm in northern Wisconsin. When she was very young, she became sick with polio. Kathryn's polio caused the muscles in her leg to weaken, and her foot became twisted. She had surgeries to straighten it, but doctors were never able to restore the foot to normal.

Like President Roosevelt, Kathryn did not let her crippled leg stop her from enjoying a full and happy life. She and her husband Paul raised seven children. She lived to be ninety-one.

The real-life inspiration for Katya, Kathryn Kozak, with one of her great-grandchildren

Kathryn Baratka Kozak was my mother.

The story DANCING WITH KATYA is a work of fiction. While the events in the story didn't actually happen, I like to think they could have.

—Dori Chaconas

Andy Rummel before he came down with polio

*O*n a hot August day in 1935, my dad Andy Rummel, who was ten at the time, was staying with friends on a Montana ranch. He rode a horse down to pick up the mail, but once he had slipped off, he found that he no longer had the strength to stand. He never ran or jumped or played baseball or rode a bike again. Dad had polio.

He spent the next four years in and out of a hospital ward for children with polio, several hundred miles from home. But my dad gained two things that I have recognized in others who survived this terrible disease: the determination to live as normal a life as possible, and a disdain for self-pity.

Although my dad suffered paralysis in both legs, he was determined to walk again—and he did. He never played ball again, but he became a coach. He never ran again, but he and his home-built car won the 1939 Montana Soap Box Derby. He even traveled to Akron to compete in the national race.

Andy, seated at left, at an Easter party in the children's polio ward of St. Vincent's Hospital

Andy in his Soap Box Derby racer

Andy and Mary Eva's wedding day, June 18, 1949

Dad was raised with a love of the outdoors, and hunting and fishing were his lifelong passions. Polio never kept him from a trout stream or a mountain meadow in elk season. And Andy Rummel made sure that his seven children were first in line to receive the polio vaccine as soon as it became available. When Dad died in 2002, he'd been married to my mother Mary Eva for fifty-three years.

—Constance Bergum